Wiffen

TERRY PARRISH

PublishAmerica
Baltimore

Hardcover 9781462674282
Softcover 9781462680146
PUBLISHED BY PUBLISHAMERICA, LLLP
www.publishamerica.com
Baltimore

Printed in the United States of America

wiffen

CHAPTER 1

Halloween night descended on Oreville with rage. A northern storm launched savage winds toward the normally quiet valley. The small town, usually active, stood like a sentinel braced for defense.

Oreville's children prepared to attack the streets with a fury of their own. Trick-or-Treating would be cut short tonight. The storm's main force was predicted to strike around midnight, and the town council, as a safety issue, had voted to enforce an eight o'clock curfew. Children must take their candy stash, it was decided, and scamper for home by the appointed time.

Darkness toward the end of October descends rapidly, and that night was no exception. The moon lay hidden beneath a blanket of clouds. Wind-tossed leaves spiraled skyward like hordes of flying insects. Shadows danced amongst the semi-barren trees casting ghostly apparitions. That night was not for the faint of heart. It had all the ingredients needed to stir superstition and fear to their heights.

The children spilled out from the protection of their homes and rushed headlong into the blustery evening. Each child, shrouded in a costume, inherited a secret identity. They scurried like mice in all directions. Time was precious, and little could be spared, since treat bags had to be quickly filled. Patience grew thin as children struck feverishly on front doors. Woe to those too slow to respond, as tiny, desperate hands banged on the front door with deafening force.

Tension mounted as parents, many remaining behind, paced the floor and anxiously awaited their children's return. Coffee and frayed nerves became silent companions as the rampaging storm roared in from over the ridge to the northwest.

It was Halloween night…when madness overshadows rationality and normalcy suddenly vanishes.

Our worst fears surface as nightmares. Demons, created through more than a million years of evolution, are beckoned from the dark recesses of the mind. They arise at night to terrorize us as they did our early ancestors. However, such intangible phantoms never materialize as real flesh and blood. Fortunately for us, they cannot escape the confines of our own minds. Yet this night defied logic. No one bothered to look at the church upon the hill, but if they had they would have noticed that the bell tower had mysteriously grown. A sharp eye might have caught a fleeting glimpse of moonlight that reflected off of eight, foot-long polished claws. Each needle point talon pierced the stout brick building as the scaled claws, squeezing from anticipation, sent small chunks of matter hurtling toward the pavement below. A hulking body squatted in silence on its man-made perch. Its brutish frame, silhouetted against a dark sky, remained undetected still. The monstrous creature from the pits of hell grew impatient as it searched for flesh during the darkest hours of night.

It nervously flicked two gargantuan wings, while the hunter's eyes easily pierced the coal-black darkness… searching…forever searching. The monstrous head suddenly craned outward and exposed its leather-like neck. Veins expanded as the hot blood surged throughout its trembling body. It caught site of movement…a red headed girl foolishly alone.

Several people had disappeared without a trace from the valley over the years. It had baffled all except one who knew the terrible secret: a crazed, old woman the town people avoided. They called her a lunatic. Older children jeered and called her a witch. Younger ones buried faces in their mother's chest when they saw her. Adults laughed and everyone scoffed at the senseless, rambling poem she recited, her eyes glistening, to everyone she met. It echoed throughout the town for many years; a warning of doom from something she called the WIFFEN.

Beware of the wiffen
In the dark of night
It lives inside a mountain
Hidden from sight
Beware of the Wiffen
When it takes flight
Stay out of the open
And away from the light
Beware of the Wiffen
No matter if you are brave
It will grab you in a second
And carry you to its cave
So beware of the Wiffen
For your body it will crave
Leaving only scattered bones
And its home as your grave

Yet no one believed her, and the people of Oreville remained ignorant to the winged demon that hid beneath the shadows of the night.

CHAPTER 2

A dark figure crept silently down the stairs; its macabre face enveloped within a black hood. "The Messenger of Death" had arrived.

A woman sat engrossed in her novel, unaware of chalk-white hands that stretched menacingly toward her exposed neck. In the room's dim lighting, the hooded figure cast an enlarged, dark shadow upon the wall. Sensing the movement at last, the woman spun around in her chair and stared directly into the face of the Grim Reaper. She flung the book to ground and screamed, "Julie, you scared me to death!"

"Isn't it a great costume, Mom?" laughed Julie. God, I love Halloween, she thought.

Julie Reagan removed her mask and hood with long-delicate hands. Flame-red hair fell past her bony shoulders and accentuated cream-colored skin. Pale-blue eyes stared forward, then fell upon a framed picture of her father, and began to mist over. A dull, empty ache chewed at her soul. Never had a twelve-year old been so troubled. Guilt and anger gnawed away at her mind. That fateful night last January would be etched in her mind forever. She was daddy's little girl and spoiled. She knew that her dad could not resist her pleading. Her demand for pizza sent her father to town during a torrid rainstorm. He never returned. His speeding jeep careened down an embankment and overturned.

The police were never able to find her father or recover his body. Footsteps were found that led away from the wreck back toward the highway, but he was never seen again. It was as if he had been removed from the face of the Earth as a chess piece is plucked from the board when captured. His strange disappearance remained unsolved.

CHAPTER 3

A rap on the door and accompanying laughter told Julie her friends had arrived. She hurried to the door as the grandfather clock chimed six times. That left only two hours to carry out her devilish plan. Tonight, the girls were to search not only for candy but also a witch. In addition to Trick-or-Treating, the crazed, old woman would be targeted.

Jill, Tina and Cassie had been Julie's best friends since first-grade. They always joined her wild escapades, and this was no different. The plan was simple…creep near the old woman, frighten her and then run. Sweet revenge for the years they had spent as young children terrified by her and the poem.

"Great costume," chimed Tina, as Julie opened the door and offered a ghoulish grin.

"You have just stared death in the face," kidded Julie.

"It is scary," giggled Tina.

"Let's hurry," whined Cassie, "We don't have much time you know." Her voice always had a whining tone to it.

"I'm leaving, Mom!" yelled Julie, but before an answer could come, the girls darted out the door. A few quick steps later they turned the corner and disappeared from sight.

The sounds of screams and laughter cut through the chilled air. Costumed children scurried and called to each other throughout neighborhoods all across town, but as curfew approached the cry of the strengthening wind reclaimed the night's solitude. Thunder rumbled in the distance, and lightning arced across the heavens revealing ominous, carbon-colored storm clouds with brief poked periods of stars.

Four costumed figures cautiously approached a darkened alley. A sudden web of lightning spread itself across the night sky and exposed a small niche ahead. A few meager belongings were strewn about the ground. An old tattered quilt lay neatly folded upon a flattened cardboard box. A shopping cart stood in the far corner filled with odds and ends that were covered by a clear plastic tarp that provided protection from the elements. These were the old woman's worldly possessions.

"She's gone," whispered Julie as she twisted to face her friends. There they stood...frozen in terror. She followed their gaze, and her eyes fixed on a bent figure that slowly approached. Barely recognizable in the glow of the distant streetlight, the ragged clothes and the rapping of a cane along a wall left no doubt in the girls' minds of who this was.

Jill, Tina and Cassie had seen enough. The three dashed down the street and left Julie standing alone. Her legs would not move, as if frozen to the ground, and only her mind raced as her eyes met the steel-gray eyes of the demented old woman. When the old woman spoke, however, it was with clarity and urgency. No poem or garbled message parted her weathered lips.

"Tonight the beast rides the wind!" Her eyes widened with fear. "I feel it watching and waiting."

A shiver traveled along Julie's spine causing the hair to stand upright on the back of her neck.

"Run, child, run!" shouted the old woman.

Panic seized her as blood rushed to her brain. Adrenaline surged throughout her trembling body, and the flight response now kicked in. Julie's heart throbbed as she bolted down the street.

"Stay clear of the open!" the old woman screeched, but her voice was muffled by the howl of wind. Julie did not hear the warning. Her feet beat a quick rhythm as she sprinted through the now deserted streets. Her ghoulish costume gave the illusion of floating as she moved. The hood bellowed as it collected air, and her mask clung stubbornly atop her head. Raindrops pelted her face. Hysteria seized her as she realized her friends' abandonment. She was ALONE!

"Why did they leave me?" she screamed inside her mind. "I'll never speak to them again!"

Fortunately, she knew a short cut home. By cutting through the ballpark, she would be there in a matter of minutes. She left the sidewalk and the cover of the tree-lined street, heart pounding, and ran out into the open expanse of the sports' park. A dark structure loomed to her right...the ball field backstop. Julie now started to cross the outfield. She kept her eyes fixed on a pool of light cast by the street lamp in front of her house.

"It won't be long now," she told herself encouragingly. "I'm so close!" Julie's lungs craved oxygen, so she slowed to catch her breath.

Birds of prey are constantly on the watch for the slightest movement, and the Wiffen was no different. The creature wheeled slowly above. It looked like a fugitive from some long lost world...dark against the moonless sky, waiting for the right moment. As Julie's pace slowed in the open field, the beast struck. It folded its bat-like wings and dropped like a stone. Sailing in with pinpoint accuracy, the Wiffen slowed, only momentarily, before its outstretched claws dealt her a savage blow. The intense force knocked Julie senseless. As she lay stunned on the ground, it alighted near her motionless body and wrapped its talons easily around her thin frame. The Wiffen catapulted skyward as her limp form dangled below the beast's titanic body. On the ground, a scattered bag of candy was all that remained.

Somewhere above the dark rugged slopes of a distant mountain, Julie's mask, which had clung so doggedly in the wind earlier, was ripped from her head. It wind milled downward until snatched by a tree branch. Here the "Face of Death" dangled several feet above the sandy soil rocking back and forth in the wind as if in celebration of a victory.

The Wiffen clutched Julie in its claws as it shot toward the distant peak and its dark cavern. Once inside the bowels of the Earth, it safely placed its prey on a ledge ringed with shear walls...there to be quickly eaten or kept alive until hunger called. The beast took special care to make escape impossible for it had lost a woman many years before. She had slithered through a fissure from its previous cave and somehow escaped its dogged pursuit. No one had escaped since; the Wiffen saw to that. This cavern has no way out for wingless creatures. They are forever TRAPPED!

CHAPTER 4

It seemed surreal, this endless highway that stretched on and on like a black ribbon. Large snowflakes moved densely and steadily, with a visible silence, in the headlights. They floated toward the windshield and were instantly sucked away into the darkness. Each oncoming car hissing by and quickly vanishing was a rarity while above lurked a vast, black undulating sea of clouds... a nasty night indeed. The town of Oreville seemed more distant than the map showed. The drone of the engine and the hypnotic effect of the wipers made time appear frozen. The endless miles took their toll and sleep beckoned. His vision blurred as signs slipped past like ghosts in an early morning fog.

Jarrod Dawson was on military leave. After eight years and two tours in Northern Afghanistan with the Army's 10th Mountain Division, he was on a personal mission, a childhood dream... a story that became infectious over the years.

Jarrod's eyes became listless and his vision trance-like. He shook his head to drive away sleep. Jarrod noticed the snowflakes had diminished and were now interspersed with rain. The darkness now seemed less inhospitable. His mind, still drunk from lack of sleep, drifted recalling the telling of the story.

His grandfather had told a tale of a vein of gold found in a cave in the mountains north of a town called Oreville. He loved his grandfather deeply and believed him. For years, Jay, as his grandfather called him, would sit wide-eyed and listen to the captivating story unfold.

"It was 1931. Sam and I staked a gold-claim in the mountains above a small mining town called Oreville. 'You boys ain't got no sense for gold', the other miners said, but they were wrong. Our claim set high on the mountain, away from the others. It was a hunch boy, a hunch, and it paid off. The area had many natural caves. Some gave us an uneasy feeling. They were pit-like...deep and foreboding, and I'm sure were a murderous trap. Others we were able to poke around in and explore with climbing ropes. It was inside one of these caves where we stumbled onto a large vein of gold, but winter's icy grip was tightening, and we had little time. A hard decision had to be made. We decided to return in the late spring and mine for the gold. Two columns of tower-like granite set above the cave's entrance; this would be our marker. It was late April when we returned only to find that an avalanche had erased all familiar signs. We never found the cave again. But it's there boy, still there, just waiting with all its riches. One day we'll go back you and me."

His grandfather's death left a deep emotional scar within Jarrod. It was his grandparents that had raised him. He never knew his father and his alcoholic mother abandoned him for a boyfriend when he was nine. Jarrod was at the old man's bedside when he died.

"I have nothing left to give you," said his grandfather, "but my story." If you find that cave, you could be wealthy beyond belief." He gave Jarrod's hand a weak squeeze then slipped into eternal night. Tears welled in Jarrod's eyes.

"I promise Grandfather, I promise," he replied in a cracking voice as he rested the now limp hand on the bed.

Jarrod emerged from the swirl of banished thoughts that invaded his mind and was startled by the sudden appearance of city lights. On his right, a well-lit road sign advertised for the Pine Motel…just ahead. He quickly turned into the nearly empty parking lot and entered the small, cramped office. Jarrod pressed the desk bell several times before an aged white-haired man with small wire-rimmed glasses and a rumpled nightshirt shuffled to the counter. Jarrod filled out the information form while the man lowered the glasses on his nose and rubbed the sleep from his eyes. He re-adjusted his glasses while Jarrod pushed the completed form toward him. He slowly turned it around and gave it a quick read. After Jarrod paid for the room, the man turned and fumbled for the room key from a wall hook then slid it across the counter.

"Room number seven," he mumbled. The manager glanced at Jarrod from over his shoulder as he shuffled back down the hall.

Jarrod walked past the rows of dark brown doors, taking a step back when he reached the end of the line to be sure that in the dim light he had the right room.

"Seven's a lucky number," he said to himself as he turned the door key. The room was small and dark and smelled of stale smoke. Its Spartan décor consisted of a small, straight-backed chair, two nightstands, a tiny dresser, and double bed made from white pine. A dingy, cocoa-brown carpet and green bedspread made the cramped room look even smaller. Exhausted from driving and thinking and unable to stay awake any longer, Jarrod fell fully clothed atop the bed and slept as the moon played the child's game of peek-a-boo from behind the clouds as the storm waned.

Sunlight streamed through the open curtains, which

highlighted dust particles suspended in the air. Jarrod awakened from his deep sleep and blinked uncontrollably as the eye-piercing shafts of light illuminated the room. The warmth felt wonderful. He was still attired in last night's clothing and realized that he had left his travel bags in the truck and rushed outside. Jarrod returned and shaved, showered and quickly dressed. A gnawing hunger in his stomach was a powerful driving force.

The crisp morning air stung as it filled his lungs. Frosted water droplets glimmered like rhinestones in the sunlight. Pine boughs hung broken and limp on the few trees that lined the parking lot; their fragrance permeated the air. Jarrod walked along the street and noticed a café sign about three blocks away. The main street was lined with turn-of-the-century buildings. They couldn't have changed much since his grandfather was here, he thought. A board walkway ran in front of the buildings and continued to the end of the street. He focused his attention northward and gazed upon the mountains for the first time. They stood shrouded in wisps of clouds. Snow-filled canyons ran like arteries down from the peaks until the lower elevation claimed their white blood.

"My god they're majestic," muttered Jarrod.

As he lowered his eyes, he couldn't help but notice a church in the distance with the bell-tower while at the same time his stomach growled in protest reminding him that he needed to start walking toward the coffee shop.

When Jarrod opened the café door, a small, brass bell attached to the interior of it clanged and signaled his presence. Several customers stared as he made his way to the rear of the café.

He was a handsome man with a face that belonged on the cover of a top fashion magazine. Blonde hair of medium length cut short along the sides, and hazel eyes enhanced his good looks. His muscular physique on a six-foot three-inch frame always turned heads.

Jarrod felt uncomfortable with the customers' stares but pushed this thought from his mind as the mingled smells of bacon and coffee reached his nostrils. He selected a corner booth away from the prying eyes of the patrons and slid onto the small bench.

As he waited for service, Jarrod wondered if all strangers to this place received such looks.

CHAPTER 5

Jarrod adjusted the cramped booth to fit his large frame by sliding the table several inches toward the opposite seat. "Much better," he said to himself as he stretched his legs. He smoothed the plastic red-and-white checkered tablecloth with his hand then drew the menu from its small wire holder. Opening it up, he mulled over the choices.

"I'm so hungry that everything looks good," thought Jarrod. He made his selection and replaced the menu.

An elderly waitress moved from behind the counter and approached him. She wore a short pink dress with ruffled sleeves and a grease-stained white apron wrapped around her waist. Her face was thin; her high, smallish forehead etched with many wrinkles. In addition, she had a sharp pointed chin and eyes like clouded blue marbles that narrowed as she approached Jarrod. He noticed that she wore a hearing aide in her left ear.

Jarrod laughed to himself because she so reminded him of his mother's childhood tale of a witch who captured little children and baked them in her oven.

"Something to drink?" she asked in a soft melodious voice.

This caught him by surprise, dissolving his expectation that a cackling sound would emerge from her narrow lips.

"Coffee," said Jarrod, "and I'll have the lumberjack special with eggs over medium, bacon, hash browns and wheat toast."

The waitress turned and walked back behind the counter where she placed the order and poured coffee into a small, silver coffeepot. She turned and, with a shaking hand, placed the pot in front of him.

"Are you here to hunt deer?" she inquired as she refilled the near empty sugar container with new packages of NutraSweet and raw cane sugar.

"Yes," replied Jarrod, as he wanted the true reason to remain a secret. Also, he needed directions, some supplies and, most of all, a way to the base of the mountain.

"Deer hunting has been poor in this area for several years," she noted, pouring Jarrod another cup of coffee as she talked. "Most folks around here believe some type of disease has pretty much wiped out the deer population in our mountains. Not many hunt here anymore," she said. The waitress then left to check on her other customers.

"Maybe she knows of a guide who can get me to the mountains?" he thought, "or if there's a sporting goods store that sells hunting and camping gear; they would surely know of someone."

Jarrod's mind raced with plans for the excursion, which were interrupted when the waitress returned with his food.

"Is there a store that sells hunting or camping gear nearby?"

"Sure," she replied, "Just make a left out the door, and its two blocks on your right. Look for Lane's Feed and Supply store."

"Thank you," replied Jarrod.

"Anything else?" asked the waitress in an obvious hurry.

"No thanks," he said, "I'm good."

The waitress placed the bill on the table and scurried away.

Jarrod was extremely hungry and wasted no time in devouring his breakfast. Licking the last of the bacon grease from his lips, he shivered with anticipation, realizing he was really doing it…he was in pursuit of his grandfather's, and his own lifelong dream.

Right after paying the bill, Jarrod left the small café not noticing if the stares that followed him in also followed him out.

It was a raw, cold day, and he pulled his collar closer to his neck. He walked slowly, enjoying the brisk, frosty morning, and wondered how cold it would get in the mountains. His chain of thought was broken when he walked through the front door of the feed and supply store.

Jarrod was struck by the aroma of hay mixed with the smell of burnt wood that came from a small, black pot-bellied stove that permeated the barn style building. Many rusted, old farming tools hung from the ceiling and walls. One wall had a large black picture with the word "BLACKSMITH" painted on it in large white letters. Near the back, a sign read, "GENERAL STORE". Jarrod walked in that direction and noticed a man stacking canned goods on a shelf.

"May I help you?" the man asked with a smile. He was a broad shouldered fellow with a round red face, a short crop of sandy hair with graying temples and a slight turned-up nose.

"Yes," replied Jarrod, "I need camping supplies but also some local information."

"Sure thing", said the man grinning. "I've lived in this valley many years and know most of what goes on around here."

"Do you know of someone who could direct or guide me to the base of the mountains? I'm willing to pay for their services."

"Are you a hunter or planning to backpack?" asked the man. He grabbed two labeled cans with pudgy hands from a crate resting on the floor and placed them next to the others on the shelf while awaiting Jarrod's answer.

"No," said Jarrod, "I'm doing a geological survey for the government," he lied.

The man hesitated for a second with a puzzled look on his face before he answered. "The most accessible way to the mountains is through the Indian Reservation. Otherwise, you will have to get back on the highway and head east about thirty miles and take the Wolf Creek exit for another ten miles until you get to Devils Creek Campground," said the man as he placed his left foot on the now empty crate. A quick straightening of his knee sent the crate sliding across the concrete floor and out of the way.

"I do have a good friend who lives on the reservation and may be able to help. As a young man, he guided for a hunting outfitter and knows the mountains well."

"That would be a great help," replied Jarrod.

The man started toward the office but then abruptly stopped and turned around.

"When do you need to go?" he asked.

"As soon as possible," replied Jarrod. The man turned and disappeared into the office.

Jarrod walked through the store, enumerating in his mind the provisions packed in his backpack. He could remember every item as he had gone over this several times making sure nothing was forgotten. By his calculations, he estimated that the supplies would have to last him about three to four days. In addition, he had a down jacket, wool clothing, and a sleeping bag guaranteed to keep someone warm up to twenty degrees below zero. He paused, for a short time, by the pot-bellied stove and placed his hands, palms down, inches away from the top warming them by the heat that still radiated from the smoldering fire.

Jarrod waited approximately ten minutes before the office door opened and the man emerged with a grin.

"My friend, Bob, said he could take you to the base of the mountains tomorrow. I'm delivering a load of hay to his ranch this afternoon and you can follow me in your vehicle," said the man. "Bob said he would leave a message at the main gate to let you on the reservation."

"Great," said Jarrod, trying to hold back his excitement.

"Bob also said you can stay at his place tonight and get an early start in the morning," added the man. "Oh, I almost forgot, his fee will be fifty dollars."

In his excitement, Jarrod forgot that his truck's engine ran roughly on the trip in and was probably in need of a tune-up. He didn't want to wait an extra day for it to be repaired.

"There is one problem," replied Jarrod.

"What's that?" asked the man.

"My truck didn't perform well on the trip in, and I don't trust it."

"I'm sure that won't be a problem," stated the man. "You can ride in with me." He flashed Jarrod a toothy grin. "I will enjoy the company, and if Bob can't give you a ride back to town when you return to his ranch just have him give me a call, and I will come pick you up."

"Thank you," replied Jarrod, who was amazed by his friendliness, unlike the irregular looks displayed by the patrons at the café. "I plan to have my truck repaired when I return."

"Where are you staying in town?" asked the man.

"The Pine Motel, in room number seven," replied Jarrod. He felt a wave of excitement and his body tingled.

"I'll pick you up around two o'clock then," said the man.

Both of them had been so engrossed in conversation that

neither one had introduced themselves. As the man started back toward the office, he stopped.

"I think it would be a good idea if we introduced ourselves. I'm Frank Lane, owner of this store." He reached out to shake hands.

"I'm sorry; that would be a good idea," said Jarrod, reaching out his own hand. "My name is Jarrod Dawson." He was angry for not introducing himself earlier, for he took pride in his military manners.

After buying a few needed supplies, Jarrod exited the store with the exuberance of a drum major high-stepping in a parade. He had not felt this much excitement in years, yet with it came a twinge of nervousness. It wasn't the danger of the unknown but the desire to prove his grandfather's story and find that cave of gold.

Jarrod felt a rush of warmth in the chilled air and knew his grandfather would be proud of him. He turned in the direction of the mountains and pumped his fist in the air in celebration.

He nearly sprinted the five blocks to his motel room to prepare for the adventure of a lifetime.

CHAPTER 6

In an old faded-green pickup loaded with hay, Jarrod and his benefactor rumbled down the graveled road. The pickup's missing rear window enabled the fragrance of hay to envelop the cab. Jarrod enjoyed the fresh scent. It reminded him of his boyhood days in Kansas.

He rested his head upon the worn seat as he surveyed his surroundings. Scrub pine and sagebrush covered hills rolled on for miles. On his left, the vast expanse gradually gave way to gray-ridged mountains.

His thoughts turned to his grandfather and the lost gold. "I know going into those mountains alone is not wise, and it may be my demise," thought Jarrod, "but I'm not afraid of death. Besides, it might be my salvation."

Jarrod looked over at Frank Lane who was whistling a soft unknown harmonious tune. The smooth melody and vibrating truck soon erased all thoughts. He closed his tired eyes and drifted off to sleep.

It seemed only a moment later that he was pulled to wakefulness by the rapid stop of the lurching truck.

"You wait here, and I'll fetch Bob Redfeather," said Frank. The truck's weathered door creaked upon rusted hinges resisting the motion, and swung mostly closed, leaving Jarrod behind.

Frank stood in front of a crudely constructed gate made

of old posts and bailing wire. He slid the wire loop that held the gate in place from around the fence post, and entered a rock-lined dirt path. A small circular cactus garden with neatly arranged cacti lay on either side of the walkway. Frank lifted himself up the front porch steps that squeaked under the added weight. He passed an old tattered red chair as he approached the partially open paint-chipped door. A scrawny tabby cat eyed him with suspicion from behind the chair then scooted across the front yard while two dogs barked in unison from somewhere behind the house. He tapped on the screen door several times and waited. Running stubby fingers through his thinning hair with one hand, he patted the perspiration from the back of his neck with the other, using a white handkerchief taken from the rear pocket of his blue overalls. The front door slowly opened, and Frank disappeared as the screen door smashed closed against its wooden frame.

Jarrod gazed at his surroundings as he sat in the old pickup. The sun-bleached adobe blockhouse reminded him of a scene from an old western movie. His eyes slowly scanned the horizon through the pitted windshield. The sky was free of dense clouds. A few scattered thin ones still floated over the distant peaks. The air now felt much warmer. The gray fangs of granite that rose from the sage covered valley floor resembled the backbone of some long-gone creature. Jarrod felt the wonders of creation with his main focus on the gray rock megaliths along the horizon and their lengthening shadows as the sun descended.

"Will I ever find gold?" he wondered.

His thoughts were wrenched from the mountains and the gold as he heard voices approaching the truck. He slid across the patched vinyl seat, stepped from the cab and was introduced to Bob Redfeather.

"Bob, I'd like you to meet Jarrod Dawson," said Frank. Bob extended out his right hand.

"Nice to meet you," replied Jarrod.

"Same here," noted Bob.

Jarrod noticed that Bob wore his smoky-gray hair parted in the middle. A ponytail extended for more than a foot down the middle of his back. It was pulled tightly back and held in place by a braided rawhide strip. A red-tailed hawk feather hung from the piece of hide. Leathery skin stretched firmly across his low forehead and the hollowed cheekbones. His broad nose bent to the right as if once broken. A few hairs emanated from his thin, pocked face.

He observed that Bob's clothing also resembled the western style. Bob wore faded blue jeans, and an open sheepskin coat revealed a red plaid woolen shirt underneath. Snakeskin boots adorned his feet. Jarrod stood speechless as he stared at his first sight of a true, full-blooded American Indian.

"Boys, I've got work to do," interjected Frank, as he walked to the back of the truck. Both Bob and Jarrod turned and watched him as he reached into the bed, adjusted a skewed bale of hay, and set Jarrod's belongings on the ground next to him. He then slipped behind the large steering wheel of the old truck. He gave a quick wave of the hand before the truck ground to a start and headed toward the barn. It maneuvered between the two corrals and scared a flock of blackbirds that chirped their disapproval of being routed from their perch on a nearby railing. The truck passed the large barn and stopped. The gears metallic teeth ground as it was thrown into reverse and backed into the barn. The truck's once chromed grill disappeared as if swallowed by the gapping mouth of the barn. The two unexpressive strangers watched and said nothing. It was Bob who broke the silence.

"Don't worry," he said, "We stopped scalping white men long ago."

This caught Jarrod by surprise and brought a smile to his face.

"I'm sorry," said Jarrod, still chuckling, "I didn't mean to be impolite."

"Grab your gear and come inside; we'll talk over coffee," said Bob.

"Great," replied Jarrod as he grabbed his backpack and followed Bob down the rock-lined pathway. Bob Redfeather was an elder tribal council representative of the Zuni tribe and practicing medicine man. He was a traditional Indian whose ideas and beliefs seemed out of place in the modern world.

Jarrod entered the front door and stared in awe at his surroundings. The room resembled a museum for Indian artifacts. Pictures of Indians who proudly stood in their tribal regalia were neatly arranged on the back wall off the room. There were arrowheads, spears, spear-points and bows throughout the room. What really aroused Jarrod's curiosity, though, were some stone figurines arranged on a shelf. Each figurine had its own unique shape. Jarrod guessed they represented some form of animal.

Bob noticed him staring at the figurines. "Those represent petrified supernatural beings from ancient creation stories," said Bob. "The Zuni's believe in creation," he explained. "According to the legend, the first humans came from four caves in the underworld, called the Lower Regions. Then the Earth's surface was a frightening place: covered with water, shaken by earthquakes and filled with beasts of prey. The Children of the Sun, out of pity for the humans, dried and hardened the Earth with lightning arrows, then touched animals to shrink them or turn them into stone. The animals that escaped were the ancestors of the animals today." Bob turned a figurine over in his hand and continued, "Some represent reptiles and birds. These are the most powerful of the beast gods, and the ones the early Zuni's feared the most." Bob placed the figurine from his hand back on the shelf and removed a larger one. He stared at it for a moment then continued. "The Children of the Sun, it is said, would curse the humans if they dishonored them by meddling in the supernatural. A large beast of prey would be released from its stone tomb to punish them, and only a weapon forged in Earth's inner fires would destroy it."

"Your collection and legends are captivating," remarked Jarrod.

"Well, that's enough of Zuni legends," noted Bob. "Come into the kitchen, and I'll finally get you that cup of coffee I promised."

"Sounds good," said Jarrod, as he followed Bob through his living room still glancing over his shoulder at the artifacts.

After the coffee was poured, Bob offered, "I understand from Frank that you want me to take you to the base of the mountains." He looked quizzically at Jarrod, "May I ask why you want to hike those mountains alone, especially at this time of the year? Surely the government wouldn't endorse this undertaking now, right when the weather gets really unpredictable. A good example was the storm on Halloween night."

"It may seem like a fool's errand, but it's something I must do," replied Jarrod. His voice was adamant and his mind seemed made up.

"There are plenty other ways to commit suicide," said Bob.

"I have my reasons," said Jarrod stoically.

"Then I'll respect that, and say no more except this," replied Bob seriously. "You may think the Indian legends are created to scare children, but something *is* happening in the mountains and the surrounding valley that has me worried… no, truly scared," warned Bob.

Jarrod noticed a look of concern spread across Bob's face, and his lips slightly quivered. "I know I said no more legends but let me tell you a few more," continued Bob. "This is the Sioux legend of Iya. Iya is a monster that is pure evil. It devours man and beast and sometimes appears in the shape of a storm." Jarrod's thoughts were drawn to the Halloween night storm but dismissed this as ludicrous.

Bob watched a fly crawl around the lip of his coffee cup. He chased it away with a sweep of his hand before continuing his monologue.

"Many North American Indian tales tell of the 'Cliff Ogre', a monster that kicks humans over a cliff so that they may be eaten by her brood. I can't leave out the Manitou; it's a manifestation of some form of power that is not from this world but comes from somewhere else." Bob paused, took a sip of coffee, and continued on. "On Halloween night, a young girl vanished from Oreville without a trace. The police found evidence that she was in a ball-field near her home when she just disappeared. It was as if she was sucked up into the sky."

"Others have gone missing over the years in the same manner," continued Bob, "including the missing girl's father. Then there is this crazy woman who, for years, has been reciting a poem about a flying beast she calls the WIFFEN, who, she claims, lives in a cave in the mountains." I think her story and all the others may be talking about the same creature, and I know I wouldn't want to be out alone in the mountains with such a fiend on the prowl." Bob offered Jarrod another cup of coffee before pouring himself one.

Jarrod sat listening half-heartedly waiting for a smile or a laugh from him, but none came. The man was dead serious.

Bob set his coffee cup back on the table and leaned back in his chair and said, "Are these just ancient stories? Yes, however, the missing people, cattle, and the crazed woman... they're real."

For his part, Bob could see that Jarrod was not taking him seriously.

"I've lost cattle over the years, and other ranchers had livestock just mysteriously disappear; some might have been taken by coyotes, bobcats or mountain lions. However, none of these predators are large enough to carry away a large steer; generally, they eat them where they lay, leaving bones behind. Now, I never find any bones, nor do the other ranchers. So where are the bones? Additionally, deer and elk are all but non-existent around here now. There used to be hundreds in this area. Many locals blame disease, but I have my own belief."

Bob noticed that he now had Jarrod's attention.

"Yes, this is no child's nightmare, for I feel it's all too real. Our mountains have a MANITOU," he said sternly.

Bob turned and stared out the kitchen window, watching the mountains in the distance with suspicion. In the fading light of dusk, he and Jarrod sat quietly with their thoughts and watched while the gray-ridged giants slowly slipped behind Earth's black blanket, merging with the night sky.

Bob slowly rose from the table and said to Jarrod, "We better turn in; it's getting late, and we have a long ride tomorrow. We'll want to get an early start in the morning."

Bob led Jarrod down a small hallway to a back bedroom.

"Make yourself at home," he said with a smile, "The bathroom is just around the corner; I'll wake you a five." He started to leave, but stopped and turned around. "I hope you don't stay awake all night thinking a lunatic is sleeping just a couple of doors down the hall," Bob gave Jarrod a wink and left.

Jarrod closed the door, placed his backpack in a corner, and a change of clothing on a small bedroom chair, undressed and lay back on the bed. He stared up at the ceiling, and a smile crossed his lips.

"Indian legends…monsters and Manitous…are just silly children's stories. How can any adult believe in such nonsense?" he wondered.

Jarrod noticed his feet hung over the edge of the bed, and realized that he absolutely dwarfed it.

"Maybe I can call on the Children of the Sun to shrink me to fit this bed," he said laughingly to himself as he reached over and turned off the light.

CHAPTER 7

The vague memory of being struck from behind, the still-searing pain, and a faint recollection of being swept upward... together these sent a shudder through Julie as she tried to fight off hysteria.

When the Wiffen had captured Julie in its claws, she had gone into shock. A depression of the entire vital process ensued. Her blood volume and pressure dropped and the pain was dulled. Shock is nature's way of easing suffering.

Julie pressed her body tighter against the wall of her small enclave, and winced from pain. Her lacerated skin was caked with blood, half-hidden beneath the tattered and torn costume.

"How long have I been here?" she sobbed, "It's so dark; I want to go home!" Julie tried desperately to understand what happened as she recalled the events that had led to her entrapment in this dark, damp prison.

The Wiffen released its grip on her as it rested on the cave ledge. A half-eaten steer lay next to Julie. Its rotting body assaulted her nostrils with the odor of decaying flesh. The beast turned its parrot-like beak downward to rip chunks of meat from the decomposing animal, turned its head upward, and swallowed them whole.

Julie trembled as her fogged mind continued to unravel the chain of events. Her tears flowed freely, unnoticed, as she vividly remembered the hot stench of foul breath and the crunch of bone as her body still teetered on the edge of shock. *She lay frozen in terror, afraid to breathe. Her eyes tried to penetrate the nearly dark interior, but could only see a vague outline of the beast. The Wiffen continued to feed as Julie fell in and out of consciousness from the horrible smell and sounds.*

When the steer was devoured, the titan lifted off the ledge. It flew in a tight circle, then upward toward the yawning hole where now countless points of light shone bright against a black background. As the Wiffen spiraled skyward, through the opening of the large sinkhole, a galaxy of lights took shape embedded in the black universe.

Julie was not ready to die. The thought of her mother being left alone and the eternal rage of guilt she placed over herself for her father's disappearance spurred her will to live. Besides there had to be a way out!

The Wiffen's lair was a large depression in the Earth's surface that had been selected for a reason. Eons before a large earthquake had exposed the cavern and natural weathering had further enlarged the opening.

The interior of the cavern was a large chamber with various sized passages leading away from its base, and the distance from the top to bottom of the cavern was over three hundred feet with the subterranean halls floored with hundreds of years of bat guano. Fed from an underground spring, water fell like rain from the many cracks in the remaining cavern ceiling. The temperature ranged from a chilly fifty to sixty degrees. It was a black, cold, and damp inhospitable world where the Sun's rays rarely penetrated.

This is where the Wiffen had taken its victims throughout the years. The ledge where Julie laid was littered with bones… both animal and human. Shredded remnants of clothing and personal items lay where the demon had ripped them from its human victims, for in the law of fang and claw, savagery and brutality show no remorse and mercy doesn't exist.

CHAPTER 8

A knock on the door awakened Jarrod from a deep sleep. "Its five o'clock," chimed Bob, breakfast should be ready in about fifteen minutes." He bolted out of bed, rushed to the bedroom window and pulled apart the curtains where he tugged on the stubborn window until it slid open with a sharp crack.

This intrusion into the early morning darkness silenced the crickets that had been chirping nearby. Jarrod smiled as he noticed the moon and stars illuminated the sky.

"Great," he thought, "Luck seems to be on my side today."

After closing the window and curtains, he walked over to the corner of the room where his gear lay. He unzipped a rather large backpack and pulled out a tightly wrapped thirty-meter coil of static climbing rope. In addition, he removed a high-beam flashlight and flicked the switch. A broad beacon of light lit up the room. Satisfied with its candle power, he placed it back in its original position inside the backpack.

Jarrod lifted the backpack and set it on the bed. He unzipped the left side pocket and with some difficulty removed a shoulder holster that held a Ruger 357 magnum pistol. After buckling the holster over his sweatshirt, he slid on an oversized windbreaker jacket with buttons, hiding the weapon.

"This may come in handy," he said to himself, as his fingers traced the irregular outline of the waffled grip.

Jarrod finished dressing, opened the bedroom door and headed down the hall toward the kitchen. He saw a large stack of pancakes, rasher of bacon, fried eggs, and coffee sitting on the table.

"Good morning," said Bob cheerfully, "I hope you slept well."

"Yes I did," replied Jarrod.

"I thought a hearty breakfast would do you good," remarked Bob, "This may be your last home cooked meal for awhile."

"Thank you," said Jarrod, "I didn't expect such a gourmet meal."

Breakfast was eaten with very little conversation, as both men seemed deep in thought. Bob cleaned his plate, dusted some bread crumbs off the table with his napkin and slid back his chair.

"Eat as much as you want," said Bob, "I'll clean-up a little; then go saddle the horses."

"Horses," Jarrod wondered to himself. His unit in Afghanistan had used pack mules to carry supplies in the mountains, but he never had to ride one.

Jarrod finished his last swallow of coffee, put his dishes in the sink and walked back to the bedroom to retrieve his backpack. He unzipped the right pocket that held Bob's fee then returned to the kitchen and exited out the side door.

Bob had two horses tied to a railing of the corral. He had just cinched the saddle on the second horse, a brown and white pinto that chewed methodically on a mouthful of hay.

Bob turned and noticed Jarrod approaching; his backpack slung across the left shoulder. In his right hand, he carried three bills neatly folded and handed them to him.

"Thank you," replied Bob, "It's been a few years since I've been paid money to be a guide. I hope you will be satisfied."

He took the folded bills without counting and shoved them deep into a front pocket of his jeans.

"Ever ridden a horse?" questioned Bob. Jarrod's brow tightened, and his mouth twisted slightly.

"Only on a carousel," laughed Jarrod nervously.

"Don't worry," encouraged Bob, "It's easy; just put your foot in the stirrup, grab the saddle horn and lift yourself up. You will be a pro in no time; a real cowboy," he laughed and slapped Jarrod on the back.

"Your horse will follow mine," explained Bob, "Just grab the reins, and go with the horse's movement; it's simple."

Bob took the backpack from Jarrod and secured it behind his own horse then turned to face him and remarked, "I think you should carry a weapon for protection. I have a 30-30 carbine-rifle you can use; it's old but reliable. Mountain lions love areas which are not frequented by humans, and there used to be quite an abundance of them around."

"No thanks," replied Jarrod, thinking it wasn't mountain lions Bob was concerned about.

"I don't think a rifle will be necessary," Jarrod said without hesitation, "I'll make enough noise to scare them off. My hunting knife will do just fine."

"I think you are making a big mistake," said Bob, shaking his head in disbelief, "But it's your life."

Bob drew the reins over his horse's head. "Let's saddle up then," he suggested, "It's going to be a long ride."

Jarrod found that mounting the horse was easy. He grabbed the reins, mounted with relative ease, and watched his horse fall in line behind Bob's large brown mare. As they headed down the road, the mountains seemed strikingly close. His eyes scanned the base of the mountains looking for a large rift or canyon that his grandfather had described.

"Find this canyon and stay to the left. The canyon will narrow near the top; the cave is somewhere beyond," his grandfather instructed him each time he told the story.

This is what Jarrod searched for as dawn crept over the horizon. He was very conscious of his surroundings, and noticed Bob had guided his horse down an unmarked trail that zigzagged through sage and scrub pines. Each pine scattered amongst the sage and boulders strewn across the ground looked the same as the next.

Jarrod was amazed at the sure-footed horses, at how cautiously they picked their steps through the obstacle course, never stumbling or faltering.

"This is a nice way to travel," he thought, as he buttoned his jacket higher to ward off the morning chill.

The sun, egg-yolk colored rose slowly, throwing orange and red streaks, fan-like, across the sky. A crown of clouds rested on the tallest peak. As the sun continued its ascent, setting in motion a new day, subtle changes in the colors became evident. Daylight brought Jarrod back to his main objective…focusing on the mountains, not the horizon.

In the clear air, they looked close enough to touch. Rocks became more numerous and larger. Jarrod was distracted by a sharp, high-pitched cry. Above the small caravan, two red-tailed hawks circled. They screamed their challenge to the intruders that had dared enter their domain.

Bob looked up and smiled at the two predatory birds. His mind wandered as he thought about the spiritual effect of nature on his people and himself. He recalled how his father gave him his strong medicine just before he died. Bob pulled a small leather pouch from where it hung around his neck hidden under his shirt as an assurance it was still there. He gently fondled the pouch, rubbing it between his thumb and two fingers, feeling the contents inside: feathers and talons from a red-tailed hawk…his fathers and now his protector.

Jarrod watched Bob pull out the pouch and caress it in his hand, by his actions he knew it contained something of value, but said nothing.

While Bob's mind poked into the past, Jarrod had re-focused on the mountains. Now, he kept lifting up in the saddle, as if adding a few inches would give a better view.

"That might be it!" Jarrod accidentally yelled out in his excitement. This short outburst snapped Bob from his daydream. He gave Jarrod a puzzled glance.

A steep, rocky gully descended down the mountain; it was pronounced, like a large wrinkle in the mountain's skin but still to distant to observe the length it extended.

Jarrod was excited and anxious to get started on his search. He groaned silently at every turn. It seemed like eternity before Bob finally pulled his horse to a halt.

"We need to rest the horses for a short time," remarked Bob. He dismounted and stretched his legs, then walked over to check the cinches on both saddles and the backpack.

Jarrod reluctantly followed Bob's example and slid off his horse then walked over to a nearby boulder and sat down.

"We should reach the base of the mountain in about an hour," said Bob, while he poured water from a large canvas bag into his hat and offered it to each horse. Jarrod took a swallow from his canteen, sloshed the cold liquid around in his mouth, then rose and strolled out amongst the sage to loosen his legs.

After about fifteen minutes, Bob mounted his mare. Jarrod walked briskly to the pinto and placed his left foot into the stirrup. The pinto took a couple of steps backward and caused him to lose his balance. He regained it by hopping on his right leg a couple of times before he was able to swing this leg over the saddle. "Finally," he muttered to himself, shaking his head and remembering it was easier the first time. Jarrod's body shuddered with anticipation as the horses started their gradual ascent to the base of the mountain.

Jarrod drifted in and out of awareness of his surroundings, in disbelief that his life-long dream might finally come true. His reverie was broken though, when he heard the sound of a snapping limb and the rustling of brush. A large jackrabbit bolted from its hiding place near the trail.

It seemed like hours before Bob stopped his horse again, this time where the terrain grew too steep and treacherous for the animals. He dismounted and Jarrod followed his lead. Bob untied the backpack from his horse without saying a word. He was strangely quiet, and his eyes avoided Jarrod's as he handed him the backpack. He finally broke the silence.

"This is a load to carry up that mountain," noted Bob. "The footing is treacherous, and it's easy to twist an ankle or break a leg. Then you would be in serious trouble." Bob gave Jarrod a concerned look. Jarrod did not reply.

Bob helped him to put on the backpack and adjust it. Once it was snug, he turned Jarrod around to face him.

"I don't know what your reason is for climbing this mountain, but I doubt if it is for the government. It is none of my business to ask why, although I still think it is suicidal," said Bob. "Take this as fatherly advice."

Jarrod made a quarter turn and just stood staring up the mountain, not acknowledging, as if he didn't hear. After a few seconds, he asked, "Does this mountain have a name?"

"Yes it does," replied Bob. He was relieved that Jarrod didn't appear to take offense to his earlier statement. "The Spanish called it Montana de Cuevas… mountain of caves.

"Well, maybe I'll do a little exploring on the side," said Jarrod. He reached out and shook Bob's hand. "Thank you for everything."

"Good luck," said Bob as he shook hands with a firm grip. "If you are not back in four days, I'll come looking for you."

Jarrod grinned then turned around and started climbing.

"Be careful of the mountain's Mani…" he began, but stopped short after recalling Jarrod's look of doubt when he described the Indian beliefs in evil spirits.

"I will," replied Jarrod as his pace quickened. He gave a thumbs-up sign without a look back.

"Thanks again," he called, as he veered toward the left side of the ever-widening gully.

Bob noticed that he moved with the quick, powerful stride of a man accustomed to climbing mountains.

Bob stood between the two horses rubbing their muzzles. He watched Jarrod disappear amongst the scrub pine and cedar trees. As his eyes scanned up to the peak, he suddenly sensed an unknown presence that sent a chill up his spine, and the hairs on the back of his neck rose and felt like tiny wires. Bob had a bad gut feeling. Did the mountain want a victim and was a fool about to be delivered?

CHAPTER 9

Julie awoke to beams of sunlight trickling from above. The rays of light inched across the cavern's interior as the sun arced across the sky, occasionally obscured by drifting clouds that caused periods of returning darkness. The location and the angle of the sun permitted sunlight to directly penetrate the otherwise ink black interior for a limited time.

She was now able to survey her surroundings. The ledge, she estimated, was approximately fifteen feet across and extended lengthwise along the cavern wall for about forty feet, then abruptly ended. Julie glanced upward, grabbed two handfuls of greasy red hair and sobbed uncontrollably. The opening to the outside world was at least fifty to sixty feet above. She was TRAPPED!

There seemed no hope for survival. In her misery, she thought to let herself walk off the ledge to her death, but had a quick change of heart upon peering over the side and down into the chasm. Julie kicked at a pile of bones near her feet sending them scattering over the side. She waited for a sound from the bottom, but heard nothing. Suddenly, a chill traveled up her backbone, and she stumbled backward in her haste to retreat from the feeling that some magnetic force from the dark void was tugging her closer to the edge.

The light was fading fast as the sun slid further toward the western horizon. Julie had to act without delay, for the Wiffen would surely return soon. Her eyes tried to adjust as the black veil of darkness crept along the cavern wall behind the ledge. She needed to find some type of safe haven now. A dark slit, low in the wall, lay along the ledge about ten feet to her right. She started a slow, desperate crawl in that direction.

As Julie pulled herself along the damp, slick ledge, she slapped aside numerous bones. She screamed suddenly but caught herself midway as the sound reverberated throughout the cavern. Not six inches from her face was a shattered human skull. She flung it aside with a shove from the back of her hand, and with an extra spurt of adrenaline, reached a fissure that sliced through the rock wall.

The fracture along the wall was narrow, but Julie had no other choice. She believed that her slim frame could squeeze through. It was too dark inside to tell how far back it extended, so Julie tossed a stone and heard it ricochet off a back wall. She judged, from the sound that it went back at least several feet.

Julie froze as an ear-piercing cry echoed up from the depths of the cavern. The Wiffen was heading her way, either from hunger or it had heard her scream.

Her instinct to survive took over. She squeezed into the small fissure without a second thought. After crawling about eight feet, she reached a solid wall. Julie slowly rose to her feet on wobbly legs. Water dripped from above landing on her matted red hair. She pressed her back against the wall and slid to a seated position. There she pulled her legs to her chest and shivered uncontrollably from cold and fear.

The Wiffen, with its bat-like wings spread wide, came to a perch on the ledge just as Julie's feet vanished within the wall. The beast, with one long spring, landed in front of the small opening. It plunged its pointed beak as far into the fissure as possible and snapped savagely. She was safe, for now, from the deadly vice-like jaws capable of ripping her apart. The grotesque titan withdrew its beak then turned its head sideways to peer inside Julie's sanctuary. A large yellow eye opened wide, and the pupil dilated to pierce through the dark void. The Wiffen spotted its prey sitting against the back wall, out of reach. Julie, however, could not see the mammoth, rage-filled eye, as the beast pressed its hulking body against the fissure, the faint light that remained stopped filtering through the crack, and total blackness engulfed her again.

CHAPTER 10

Human life is fragile and Julie felt little hope now that hers would last much longer. She was gradually losing her will to live. The ink-black darkness and the intense hunger pangs that knifed through her stomach weakened her resolve to survive. She had found a few pieces of candy that had been stashed inside the only intact pocket of her ragged costume and had eaten them sparingly. These did nothing to ease her hunger or restore her strength. Water was plentiful, but had a strong bitter taste. The high concentration of lime caused her intense stomach cramps.

The Wiffen ruled the night. In the black emptiness of the cavern, Julie could hear and sense its presence on the ledge guarding its lost meal. Its talons clicked against the granite overhang each time it moved to observe its trapped prey. The creature was vigilant.

It was during the third day in the cavern when the sun's rays gave ample light to see but offered little respite from the constant bone-piercing cold that penetrated through her scant tattered clothing that Julie again emerged. She chanced that the creature avoided light and was deep within its dark lair. Desperation forced her outward in search of something edible and some semblance of warmth. With sunlight, came renewed energy and hope.

Julie remembered studying caves in school. Certain

creatures, she recalled, could adapt to this dark world. They were called troglodytes and most were slow moving, pale in coloration and blind. Salamanders, frogs, millipedes, cave crickets and bats came to mind. Although the thought of sinking her teeth into the body of one of these creatures repulsed her, she had no other recourse. She needed protein to regain her strength...even uncooked meat. She now had to become like her captor.

Now with the light, she might find food...STARVATION was not an option. In addition, she might find a way to the top. As Julie forced her chilled, pain-ridden body along the ledge, evidence of the Wiffen's carnage was abundant. She carefully chose a path around the bones and skulls of animals, many of which had horns. In addition, the creatures spoor with its putrid odor seemed stronger than before and brought her again to the verge of nausea as she skirted its defecation. Julie crawled slowly on shaking arms and knees, bruised and caked with dried blood, toward an area where bones were fewer. These bones appeared smaller and more scattered.

It was barely visible as it was partially covered by remnants of what looked like some type of fabric. Julie's gaze was transfixed as she ran her hand over soft leather.

"My god, it's a wallet!" she cried out but only in her mind this time.

Her hunger and bone-chilled body deserted her for the moment, and she limped back along the same path taken earlier. It was a slow process and the light was fading fast. She reached the small opening carved in the solid granite wall and stopped at the entrance...her prison within a prison.

Julie's shriveled fingers fumbled to open the scarred brown wallet and divulge its contents. For the moment, this was her only connection with humanity. The morbid fate of its owner was forgotten for now.

Dampness in the cave had caused the ink to run making the writing on the slips of paper in the wallet-fold illegible and had claimed the faces on what were probably once family pictures. Julie probed underneath a flap of the wallet and felt hard plastic, most likely a driver's license. She slowly drew out the waterproof document and stood to make better use of the fading light. Her knees buckled and her mind spun as her legs collapsed sending her sprawling on the hard surface as she recognized her father's face. All sense of reality deserted her as she moved numbly back into the far recesses of her prison, where even the numbness of dissociation was interrupted by the eternal drip, drip, drip of water leaking from above.

For many minutes, she stood in a trance while her mind, spinning like a wheel out of control, kept reliving the horror story. Julie cried hysterically, her tears fell like rain and mingled with the water that continually flowed at her feet.

Her mind, twisted from powerful emotions, continued to torment her...shear walls, starvation, jet-black darkness, bone-chilling cold and the realization of her father's brutal death sapped any will left to live. She walked a fine line between sanity and insanity. Julie could take no more and prayed only for a quick death.

CHAPTER 11

Jarrod was elated as he made his ascent along the edge of the canyon. Bob and he had crossed a stream earlier, and now he heard it gurgling as the force of gravity pulled it down from the horn of the mountain.

Thinking of Bob, he turned and watched two miniature horses and a speck of a rider moving away at a fast pace in the distance. He began, almost for the first time in his life, to feel lonely. Looking skyward, though, he smiled to think that his grandfather had been on this same mountain all those years before and hoped his spirit was by his side.

The sun beat down on the south side of the mountain, but the breeze still had a chill to it. Jarrod figured that the dusting of snow from the Halloween storm would melt quickly and not slow him down.

Jarrod wanted to reach the ridge that ran perpendicular to his course before dusk. His destination seemed relatively close. However, he knew that perception of distances can be deceiving and the steep trek grueling. The nearly four thousand foot climb would not be easy.

The ground began sloping, steeply, and though he panted and mopped his forehead a good deal, he trudged onward. His warm clothing was now a burden.

"It's hard to go so slowly when a voice inside you says hurry, hurry, hurry!" he thought to himself.

There was no trail to follow, and the terrain became more treacherous. It was rugged with numerous plants full of sharp spines. Many large boulders blocked his path requiring him to climb and clamber. Large slides of loose shale sapped away his strength. Even though he was in great shape, Jarrod's leg muscles cramped and burned.

Jarrod continued to ascend but his movement was slowed. After some hours, each step became an effort of mammoth proportion. His nostrils flared and his lungs craved more oxygen. With his energy depleted, he was forced to rest. He headed for a large boulder and for shade.

Buzzards floated above the canyon on thermal air currents. They circled overhead then moved on. Jarrod rested several minutes then angled toward the sound of running water.

He looked out over the gorge and down to the water, not fifteen feet below. Here he noticed a pool created from a logjam. Reaching down to his feet, he grasped a stone and with a flick of his wrist sent it hurtling out over the pool and into space. It floated silently through the air, then fell and disappeared, engulfed by the thick brush below.

Jarrod approached the edge of the pool, removed his backpack and sweat-soaked shirt, and lay face down on the moist soil. Inches from the ground the pungent, wet earth smelled wonderful. Here he filled his canteen and drank greedily the cold, clear liquid. He cupped his hands in the water, scooped up several handfuls, and splashed it on his face. After a few minutes, he rose on aching legs, sat down with his back against a rock, and removed his boots and changed his wet socks.

As Jarrod scrambled from the canyon, he felt re-energized, and his destination, a ridge ahead, seemed reachable before dark. There he would make camp for the night. He headed out whistling a tune.

The orange glow of the sunset slipped behind the mountain as he climbed, and with several short rests, he reached the ridge. Here he selected a sheltered area amongst a few scrub pines behind a small knoll. Jarrod unrolled his sleeping bag then removed two energy bars from a small side pocket of his backpack.

"Dinner at its finest," he laughed.

He dropped onto the sleeping bag in an exhausted state, ate the energy bars, and stared up at the night sky.

The night, marked by increasing winds and drifting clouds, created an eerie sight superimposed against the moon. Jarrod crawled inside his sleeping bag; in the chilled air, the warmth felt wonderful now.

He was awakened by two blue jays squabbling over some prized insect each one wanted. Jarrod rubbed his eyes and yawned.

"I can't remember the last time I slept so well," he thought.

He looked at his watch...it read seven-thirty. This was later than he wanted to start. He had planned on making coffee and breakfast on his small camp stove, but instead opted again for nutrient bars.

The wind had died, and the clouds were gone. Today's weather looked nice; it was a fine day to search the area. He would use this site as his base camp. Jarrod hurriedly pitched his two-man tent, stored his unneeded gear inside, and decided which direction he would take.

He climbed up the small knoll and viewed a large outcropping of rocks about a quarter mile away. Jarrod sprinted back to his camp, grabbed his canteen, flashlight, climbing rope with foot-loops and the shoulder holster with the pistol inside.

The terrain away from the gorge was easier to negotiate. He pushed the nagging soreness from his muscles to the back of his mind and moved along at a rapid pace. After about an hour, he reached the base of the rocks and within minutes of searching found an easy route to the crest of the escarpment. Here he could have a good view of the area.

Jarrod's breath was taken away by the vastness that spread before him. The irregular plateau tapered into a vast valley. Below the sun-bleached grasses, mixed with thick brush and dotted every now and then by scrub pines ringed with patches of snow were interspersed with watering holes that sparkled like diamonds in the sunlight. A few craggy rock formations metamorphosed from the Earth's underbelly formed a formidable barrier on his right. Slowly, like the hands of a clock, he turned and looked for any sign that might suggest a cave. About one-quarter of the way around, he stopped. Not far off, the ground was slightly cupped. A large number of boulders that had been cracked by the wind and extreme temperature changes seemed to have fallen from the escarpment above it. They were strewn about the brush and trees like broken pillars in an ancient lost temple.

"Could these be the granite pillars that stood above grandfather's cave and were destroyed in the earthquake?" Jarrod wondered.

A wide swath of assorted rocks, obviously gouged-out from the face of the escarpment, ran down and stopped just short of his destination. He shaded the sun from his eyes with his right hand to get a better look. In the center of the indentation, lay a large black patch.

"That could be a cave!" he exclaimed aloud, as his mind whirled from excitement, "and there's obviously been an avalanche at one time."

Jarrod scrambled off the rock out-cropping, half slid down an embankment, leaped over the stones that littered his path, skirted the larger boulders like a running back dodging tacklers, and covered the remaining distance with a final burst of speed. He paused briefly to catch his breath where the earth dipped down and gawked at the gaping hole that lay before him.

After angling downwards several feet, the ground leveled off for a brief stretch before giving way to emptiness. Jarrod edged cautiously to the lip, at last on hands and knees crawling only an inch at a time. He flattened himself against the ground as he peered over the edge into the black gulf. There was no telling how deep it might be, and the walls were sheer.

"This could be the area Grandfather described, but this cave seems to have no easy way in...one of those murderous pits he mentioned," thought Jarrod," but I'm here so I might as well check it out."

Jarrod pushed the button of the powerful flashlight. The darkness cracked with the explosion of light. Its far-reaching beam penetrated the darkness for a good distance down then illuminated the walls as it scanned. Neither a bottom nor a way down was to be found. As the beam moved along the rock face, it fell upon a ledge that jutted out of the granite wall. Jarrod's arm motion froze focusing the light on his discovery.

"A ledge!" he said excitedly.

He noticed a lifeless tree, twisted and blackened, as if once struck by lightning that balanced precariously near the precipice but directly above the ledge. Its gnarled roots, exposed to the wind over the years, had little soil. Jarrod moved at a snail's pace the short distance until he reached the out-of-place tree. He tested the tree's stability with a good shake; it moved slightly with a sharp cracking sound of dead wood. He knew this was not a safe anchor. Instead he opted for a good sized rock a little farther away.

Jarrod secured his rope around the base of the rock. He checked each foot-loop of the climbing rope before casting it over the side. As unstable sand clinging to the lip of the precipice fell like rain, the rope dropped. It found only empty space. After three more tries, the rope slackened as it hit the ledge with a rattle.

Jarrod again shined his flashlight onto the ledge wondering what had caused the abnormal sound. The rope appeared to be resting amongst a pile of bones.

"Poor dumb animals," he thought to himself shaking his head.

The fear of the unknown is a weak link in the human mind. The animal bones, dark void, and Bob's stories of Indian legends suddenly rushed through Jarrod's mind, hair prickled along the base of his skull, and his palms beaded with sweat. He had to look away to get back in control of his emotions. In Afghanistan, he had taken greater risks against real villains. Jarrod ignored this brief moment of weakness and readied himself for the descent.

He secured the flashlight to his belt, adjusted his shoulder holster, and again tested the rope with his weight then placed his right foot into the first loop. Knowing his equipment was in good working order; he pushed doubt aside, and began his descent into the dark world.

CHAPTER 12

Bob watched Jarrod snake his way up the mountain slope. His eyes followed the canyon as it twisted its way up from the desert floor and through a series of waterfalls that poured over sheer faces of granite; themselves headed for the valley below. A sense of betrayal tore at his heart.

"I should have insisted to go with him," Bob said to himself, as he watched Jarrod disappear over a ridge of the rugged terrain. "He's climbing alone and unafraid to knock on the Devil's door, and the Devil will answer."

He started ruminating about his heritage and about how the Indian people had changed over the years. "So much," he worried, "is disappearing, so much is being lost: the food, the dance, the customs and legends. I know it is impossible to forgo change, but change is not always for the better. Many Indians live a pathetic existence now with alcoholism and poverty. The old ways are better.

Bob looked back up the mountain and spoke out loud as if addressing it personally. "I know your hiding something evil up there somewhere and, it exists only to kill." He again thought about the story of the Manitou legend.

Anyone who heard the rumbling from the canyon would say it was merely the wind howling through it. But the elders believe the Manitou is growling at them from its rock home, from which it releases evil spirits down the canyon every evening.

"Maybe the mountain's Manitou is not a spirit but truly alive, Bob mused to himself. "That crazy woman in town tells of a flying beast and something is definitely not right in our valley. Whatever it may be, it needs to be destroyed, but I must do it as my ancestors would have and remove the curse," he muttered, almost as if in a trance. If anyone had a reason to conquer the mountain, it was surely Bob for there was one story he kept locked up in his mind and never told anyone outside his family.

Bob's great-great uncle, a respected shaman of his tribe, was called "Crooked Eye," so named because he was born with one eye that constantly wandered. The legend of Crooked Eye was told around many campfires. He had left his village on a short quest to gather medicinal plants. During his travels, he came upon a broken down wagon. Inside were two dead white settlers. He rummaged through their belongings and took a blanket to ward off the evening chill. Unknown to Crooked Eye, the settlers had died from a deadly influenza, and by taking that blanket he became a carrier of the disease.

Not long after Crooked Eye arrived back at camp, many members of the tribe contracted the disease and died, but he never became sick. His tribe, believing he had somehow lost his soul to evil spirits while on the journey, banished him, as punishment, to the mountains. The new medicine man put a curse on Crooked Eye and all his family members. This curse, however, came at a price. The Children of the Sun, angered by human meddling in the spirit world, unleashed an ancient beast from its stone tomb in the underworld.

Bob now knew what he must do. Only a member of the cursed family could remove this Manitou, and that was he. If this beast existed, then only a certain weapon could be used. A spear with its obsidian point fired in Earth's oven and spewed forth as through a whale's blowhole to cool and harden on the planet's floor. This weapon of early man with its deep-black radiant rock, according to the legend, when plunged into an ancient beast's lifeblood would kill... as a SILVER BULLET slays a werewolf.

Bob felt a huge sense of relief as this burden that he carried with him for so long suddenly vaporized. He spurred his horse into a quick trot as the pinto trailed behind. Time was of the essence. He figured Jarrod would have a five to six hour head start. It would take this long to get back to the ranch, unsaddle his horses, grab a quick bite to eat, a fresh mount, and prepare himself for battle then return to Jarrod's starting point. There should still be an hour or more of day-light, and a white man leaves an easy trail to follow.

He reined the mare to a stop in front of the stables, unsaddled both horses, slapped them on the rumps to hurry their entrance and closed the gate. This done, he entered the ranch house through the side door and walked into the living room. There on the wall was the weapon; his great-great uncle's ceremonial spear kept and preserved to look like the day it was made. It was seven feet in length, dyed red from the juice of crushed cactus apples, and near the end were three white circular rings placed about three feet apart. The three rings represented: humans, animals, and the spirit world. In addition, several red-tailed hawk feathers adorned the spear two and a half feet above the obsidian point. Bob entered his bedroom and exited ten minutes later wearing a buckskin outfit. On his feet, he wore moccasins for stealth. It truly looked like he stepped out of the Old West. Now ready for his quest, he grabbed a little food and rushed to the corral…spear in hand.

A saddle was not needed for this second horse, as Bob

was an excellent bareback rider. He quickly slid the bridal over the horses head, placed the bit in its mouth and cinched it down. Grabbing the horse's mane, he flung himself upon its back, jerked the horses head with the reins in the direction he wanted to go then kicked it in the ribs with his heels. The horse was agile and glided easily over the sagebrush terrain.

When the horse climbed out of the arroyo, Bob had reached the area where Jarrod had made his ascent. His tracks were easy to follow. After turning the horse loose to graze, Bob followed the boot prints. He moved effortlessly as he was not burdened by weight and made good progress.

As the weakened sun lapsed beyond the horizon, the wind took on a bite. Bob figured he would reach Jarrod by late afternoon tomorrow if he could maintain this pace. Feeling confident and full of life he could have continued on longer but traveling in the dark was not an option. He selected a small alcove that provided shelter from the wind and built a small fire. His buckskin outfit would retain much of his body heat, and keep him warm during the night where the temperature would fall below freezing. As darkness settled around him, he mentally prepared himself for what he might encounter the following day.

Like a post-card image, the sunrise painted the sky as the sound of chanting broke the morning tranquility. Bob followed an ancient ritual that gave strength and courage to his people when they were about to face an enemy. He also relinquished his Christian name, taking on his Indian name, Stalking Wolf. This name was given to him at the age of sixteen after returning from his spiritual quest for manhood. He had devised an uncanny trick for stalking deer by covering himself with mud and charcoal then topping it with natural debris. In this way, he became part of the earth. Several times stealth and concealment allowed him to get close enough to pull the hair from a deer's tail.

It was Stalking Wolf who emerged into the early morning light, his face covered in charcoal and ash from his fire. He proceeded to the stream where he spread mud over his body and grabbed handfuls of grass and small twigs. The natural vegetation would adhere to the mud when it dried.

After preparing himself, he continued to follow Jarrod's trail as it snaked toward the ridge above. This odd looking intruder covered with mud and grass seemed out of place as he moved amongst scattered scrub pines and rock piles unaware of another intruder close by. The "Mask of Death" that had dropped from the sky Halloween night hung from its host as if placed there by some demonic hand. The two hollowed eyes of the Grim Reaper faced toward the Wiffen's lair as if waiting for a deciding battle between good and evil.

CHAPTER 13

Jarrod placed each step warily as he felt for the next loop in the rope. One wrong step and he would fall over fifty feet to the ledge below. It was a slow, tricky descent, but finally he neared his destination.

He breathed out slowly and deliberately to ease his nervousness, but no longer did he think terrible thoughts of what might lie below. In fact, now it all seemed rather comical.

The angle of the sun had reached the point where its rays somewhat relieved the darkness of the cavern. Jarrod's eyes took time to focus in the dim light. Two more steps and he would reach the ledge.

As his left foot made contact with the solid surface, he took a deep breath and expelled the pent-up air. Filled with anticipation, he turned his gaze along the floor of the ledge. He removed his flashlight and flicked the switch. Its powerful beam shot outward. Rubbing the thick stubble forming on his jaw, Jarrod followed the course of the beam as it swept along the ledge, periodically stopping as it fell upon rubble after rubble of bones.

The magnitude of the carnage was impressive. In addition, a foul odor lingered about the cavern. He hadn't seen any decaying flesh still attached to the bones. A thought came to him that it could be bat guano. As Jarrod moved the light about, he envisioned the morbid little mammals with their sinister reputation. Then he reached under his jacket and unhooked the strap that held the pistol in the holster.

"A lot of good this would do against bats," Jarrod laughed out loud as he pictured about how comical that would look. He had not realized how completely silent this dark world was until his laugh reverberated throughout the cavern ten-fold.

It was shortly after the laugh that he heard it; a muffled sound that seemed to come from within the rock wall. Jarrod slid his hand toward the pistol and extracted the weapon. Both hands worked in unison as the barrel of the pistol followed the flashlight's beam toward the origin of the noise. It came from a jagged slit in the cavern wall. Something was moving within a dark hollow. Worse still, something was coming out. His trigger finger tensed against the tempered steel as Julie crawled out. As the intense beam of the flashlight fell upon her, she rose to her knees and threw her hands up to shield her eyes. The days of darkness had caused her to be like the creatures of the night. Jarrod stepped backward then stood transfixed for several seconds before lowering the beam from her face. Surely his mind was playing tricks on him. This could not be a real child but a hallucination.

Julie dropped her hands then rose and stood zombie-like. Her sunken eyes fixed on him with a blank stare.

Jarrod had a hard time comprehending what had just happened. He stood, gun still in hand, waiting for reality to return. But this seemed real not a hallucination, and a young girl, in very poor condition, stood before him.

Julie staggered forward stiff-legged and collapsed at his feet. Her arms shot outward octopus-like and held his leg in a vise grip as intense shaking and sobbing erupted from within her as she clutched her rescuer.

Jarrod stared down in disbelief. With a gesture of

consolation, he reached down and patted her head still expecting this to be an illusion created in his mind. As he felt human hair and a skull, tears leaked from his hazel eyes and slid down his cheeks then dropped from his angular jaw.

"I don't know how you ended up here or for how long," said Jarrod, his voice vibrating from emotion, "but judging by your appearance it's been awhile." His voice cracked as he tried to spit out the words. "Can you talk?"

Julie lessened her grip and raised her head. Fear radiated through her soiled face and her mouth opened, but no words came; she knew something that he didn't, but terror had muted her.

"Let's get out of here," said Jarrod as he tried rubbing some grime from her face, "It's a long way back, and you need medical attention."

Jarrod reached down, placed a hand under each armpit and gently stood her upright. He carefully guided her through the graveyard of bones to the rope. Upon reaching it, he set his pistol on the ledge, hooked the flashlight back on his belt then placed her right foot in the first loop.

"I'll be behind you. Don't be afraid; I won't let you fall," he said as he patted her leg for support.

Julie had to navigate sixteen more foot loops and in her weakened condition climbing approximately fifty feet made it an arduous task. Jarrod had to guide each alternating foot into the next loop as he kept urging her upward.

"That's it; good girl," he encouraged as each foot loop was reached.

The pace was slow but steady. The little light that filtered down from above increased the danger, but Jarrod needed both hands so the flashlight was not an option. Everything went well until about five feet from the lip when Julie froze.

"Keep going, don't stop! Just a few more feet," said Jarrod with a tone of urgency.

Julie had kept her eyes glued to the cavern wall. Then she glanced upward and saw the bleeding sunset…PANIC! Twilight was fast approaching and what came with it. She was no longer mute.

"We have to get out of here!" cried Julie hysterically. She gulped air with her mouth wide open… a sure sign of fright.

"It's Ok, just hold on we're near the top," Jarrod replied calmly trying to subdue the terror ridden girl.

Julie acquired a sudden burst of energy spurred on by a shot of adrenaline. She navigated the remaining loops on her own. Her arms shot above the lip and grasped a limb from the gnarled tree. It cracked again but held. With a shove from below from the puzzled Jarrod, she cleared the final hurtle, crawled a few yards then sprawled on her back staring skyward; eyes glazed over, as a cool rush of air nudged strands of matted red hair across her face.

Jarrod scrambled out from the cavern and pulled up the rope. He gathered it in a loose bundle and flipped it near the rock where it was anchored then walked over to check on Julie who was now sitting upright. Her head moved robot-like, scanning the sky and cavern opening; her eyes darting every direction. She was obviously looking for something noticed Jarrod.

"Are you Ok? What are you looking for?" Jarrod asked, but Julie never responded and her behavior never faltered.

Jarrod strode over to the boulder and slid the loop up over the rock. He untied the rope and was in the process of winding it into a compact bundle. Then he heard it. Faint at first, but with growing intensity. It was emanating from inside the cavern. The shrill sound bounced off the sheer walls and echoed upward; it was now ear-piercing. A banshee-like scream that split the air as an arrow flies from a bow.

Jarrod shot a puzzled glance in Julie's direction. She sat mortified, mouth again wide open. Her body shook so uncontrollably that the fine powdered sand vibrated around her.

The Wiffen had heard the two humans as they exited the confines of its lair. The light from the outside world was ebbing, and now it shot upward through the cavern's darkness like a missile.

When Julie heard the sound, she knew the horror that approached. A primal scream rose from her lungs as she ran, staggered and fell, regained her feet then wedged her body between two large boulders. She pulled her knees to her chest and rocked back and forth; her soiled face paled from shock as she covered her ears with her hands and her body stiffened.

Jarrod stood motionless as this demon from the underworld cleared the cavern's throat and rose skyward, turned and bore down upon him with talons outstretched. With the agility of a stunt man, he dove sideways under the scanty protection of the dead tree, thereby avoiding certain death. He eyed the beast as it dropped lightly to earth not fifteen feet in front of him, blocking any escape in that direction and behind him stood the gaping entry to the cavern. He was CORNERED.

He searched frantically for a solution, wide-eyed at the rasping sound the beast's wings made as they raked along the ground. Jarrod had forgotten about his pistol in the chaos and reached for it; it was GONE!

In his haste to rescue Julie, he had neglected to replace the pistol in its holster when he laid it on the ledge to place her foot in the first loop of the rope. Without it, his fate looked grim. Jarrod reached down, found a rock that fit his hand, and prepared to face impossible odds. As the beast clicked its beak and its wing joints snapped from the hurried pull of its chest muscle, he raised the rock into the air and waited...David verses Goliath.

But fate works in strange ways. Jarrod was awestruck by the strange scene that unfolded even as he cocked his arm to throw. As if a magician used sorcery to materialize a champion and slay the dragon, a mud-caked figure levitated from the earth as a moth escapes from its cocoon. With spear raised, Stalking Wolf charged forth as if spat through a time tunnel into the future; his eyes flared wide as he thrust the spear deep into the soft tissue of the beast's underbelly. The sharpened obsidian point entered with a sound like that of a knife piercing a watermelon.

There was a sudden silence as if the whole world hushed and watched. As the winged demons warm blood spurt outward from the wound with every heartbeat into the cool air, a plume of steam followed. The creature screamed its challenge with yellow eyes glaring, but now anger was tinged with pain. The Wiffen's titanic body twisted and turned upon the ground driving the now broken spear deeper into its vital organs, and its wings bent under the weight. Locked in both claws that pierced his fragile armor was a muddied human figure that struggled in vain to avoid the flesh-tearing beak. Crimson-red that flowed so freely between the two combatants turned garnet-colored as it fell to the soil in the fading light.

The battlers tumbled to the brink of the gaping hole. The savior suddenly hung limp as a chunk of the lip gave way under the stress of the added weight and both beast and human plummeted into the dark abyss.

Jarrod, rock still in hand, recovered his senses as the pair disappeared, swallowed by the earth. He walked in bewilderment across the battle scene trying to make sense of what just happened. Blood, spread like a blanket upon the ground, mingled with the earth. A few more steps and he reached the gouged-out section where the battle ended. There, resting only six inches away from oblivion was a small leather pouch. This was the same pouch that Bob had been holding in his hand on the horseback ride in. Now it was obvious who had saved their lives.

"Bob didn't wait the three days," Jarrod said to himself, "He came early. Why, I'll never know. He must have had a sixth sense which warned of the creature," he glanced over the lip, "Bob took the answers to the grave with him."

He turned the leather pouch around in his shaking hand and pulled open the raw hide pull-string that kept it closed. When he saw the parts from the red-tailed hawk, he knew it had something to do with his Indian beliefs. He thought of the Indian's spirit world and the legends that Bob told and how one came true. Jarrod re-tied the pouch then tossed it over the edge and watched the rawhide strips tied around the neck flap behind the pouch as it sailed through the air before it disappeared forever through the doorway to the Underworld.

"May this protect you in your spirit world," said Jarrod in a slow deliberate tone. He was saddened by the loss of his guide and savior but changed his focus as he remembered Julie was still in hiding.

Jarrod turned and briskly walked toward Julie who was forgotten during the chaos. She still remained wedged between the two boulders even though she had witnessed the battle and knew her horror was over.

As Jarrod walked over to Julie who was now just extracting herself, he thought back over his reason for coming here in the first place… his grandfather's story of the lost gold mine. It was a lifelong dream, something you think you may grasp, but when you reach out it's gone in a fleeting moment. He looked toward the heavens. Clouds slipped across the evening sky, and the first drops of rain began to fall.

The air had become very still during the combat. Just as suddenly as the battle ended, the evening rustled with a soft breath of air, as if created by some celestial intervention. It traversed the battleground and flowed down the mountain.

The tree branch that held the "Mask of Death" for so long swayed in the light breeze and released its grip on the intruder. The mask twirled earthward and landed, face down, atop the sandy soil. Immediately, grains of sand began to filter through the hollows of the mask. This began the slow process of being buried under Earth's blanket as a symbol of the triumph of good over evil.

Back up the mountain, two figures stood along the crest of the ridge outlined against the horizon. The small figure had one arm around the larger one's waist. Both stared at a faint glow far down in the valley; each with an incredible story to tell. Then as the gray veil of clouds lowered across the mountain's face, they vanished like two phantoms in a London fog.

Would you like to see your manuscript become a book?

If you are interested in becoming a PublishAmerica author, please submit your manuscript for possible publication to us at:

acquisitions@publishamerica.com

You may also mail in your manuscript to:

PublishAmerica
PO Box 151
Frederick, MD 21705

We also offer free graphics for Children's Picture Books!

---

www.publishamerica.com

CPSIA information can be obtained at www.ICGtesting.com
Printed in the USA
BVOW08s0431150515

400394BV00024B/5/P